ASTRA & APOLLO

TAE KWON DO
CHAMPS

BY
V.T. BIDANIA

ILLUSTRATED BY
EVELT YANAIT

PICTURE WINDOW BOOKS
a capstone imprint

For Owen —VTB

Published by Picture Window Books,
an imprint of Capstone
1710 Roe Crest Drive
North Mankato, Minnesota 56003
capstonepub.com

Library of Congress Cataloging-in-Publication Data
Names: Bidania, V.T., author. | Yanait, Evelt, illustrator.
Title: Astrid and Apollo, tae kwon do champs / by V.T. Bidania ;
illustrated by Evelt Yanait.
Description: North Mankato, Minnesota : Picture Window Books,
[2022] |
Series: Astrid and Apollo | Audience: Ages 6-8. | Audience: Grades
K-1. | Summary: Astrid and Apollo really want to win their events
at the tae kwon do competition, but when things do not go according
to plan, the twins discover there is more than one way to become a
winner. Includes facts about the Hmong.
Identifiers: LCCN 2021002465 (print) | LCCN 2021002466 (ebook) |
ISBN 9781663908759 (hardcover) | ISBN 9781663920188 (paperback) |
ISBN 9781663908728 (ebook pdf)
Subjects: CYAC: Twins—Fiction. | Brothers and sisters—Fiction. |
Hmong Americans—Fiction. | Tae kwon do—Fiction. | Competition—
Fiction.
Classification: LCC PZ7.1.B5333 Ax 2022 (print) | LCC PZ7.1.B5333
(ebook) | DDC [E]—dc23
LC record available at https://lccn.loc.gov/2021002465
LC ebook record available at https://lccn.loc.gov/2021002466

Designer: Kay Fraser

Image credits: Capstone/Dara Lashia Lee, 61; Shutterstock: Ingo
Menhard, 60, Yangxiong (pattern), 5 and throughout

Table of Contents

ASTRID GAO NOU

Hi, I'm Astrid. My twin brother is Apollo, and we were born in Minnesota. We live here with our mom, dad, and little sister, Eliana.

Hi, I'm Apollo! Our mom and dad were both born in Laos. They came to the United States when they were very young and grew up here.

APOLLO NOU KOU

MOM, DAD, AND
ELIANA GAO CHEE

gao **(GOW)**—girl; it is often placed in front of a girl's name. Hmong spelling: *nkauj*

Gao Chee **(GOW chee)**—shiny girl. Hmong spelling: *Nkauj Ci*

Gao Hlee **(GOW lee)**—moon girl. Hmong spelling: *Nkauj Hlis*

Gao Nou **(GOW new)**—sun girl. Hmong spelling: *Nkauj Hnub*

Hmong **(MONG)**—a group of people who came to the U.S. from Laos. Many Hmong from Laos now live in Minnesota. Hmong spelling: *Hmoob*

Nou Kou **(NEW koo)**—star. Hmong spelling: *Hnub Qub*

tou **(TOO)**—boy or son; it is often placed in front of a boy's name. Hmong spelling: *tub*

CHAPTER 1

Trophy Shelf

"Heeyah!" Astrid yelled loudly and kicked as high as she could. She liked doing kicks at tae kwon do class. Master Leon said Astrid's yell was the strongest yell in the class!

Snap! The board that Master Leon held cracked in half as Apollo punched it. That was Apollo's favorite part of tae kwon do class. The boards may have only been made of foam, but Apollo broke them on the first try every time!

When class came to an end, Astrid and Apollo sat down on the mat with the other students. They were all excited. Master Leon had said he had good news to share. Everyone was curious to hear what it might be.

"Class was fun!" Apollo said. He wiped his forehead.

Astrid fixed her ponytail. "Yes! Let's practice more at home tonight!"

Apollo nodded. "I wonder what Master Leon wants to tell us."

Master Leon took his place at the front of the room.

"Students, you did well today. I want to tell you about a special event coming up. Our class is going to a tae kwon do tournament!" he said.

"A tournament?" Astrid, Apollo, and the rest of the students gasped and cheered.

"You will compete in forms, board breaking, and sparring. You will have the chance to win awards. It will be a very good day!" he said. "Your parents are here now. I will see you at the next class."

The students stood up. They bowed to Master Leon.

Astrid and Apollo saw Dad by the door. They put on their shoes and hurried over to him.

"How was class?" asked Dad.

"It was fun!" said Astrid.

"We're going to a tae kwon do tournament!" said Apollo.

Dad smiled. "That sounds great. Tell me more in the car. I need to pick up something from Auntie Xai."

Astrid and Apollo were very excited about the tournament. They talked about it on the way to the car, as they got into the car, and all the way to Auntie Xai's.

Soon they were at Dad's sister's house. Dad parked in front.

Apollo stopped talking about the tournament. "What are we picking up?" he asked.

"Auntie Xai found a shelf from when we were kids. I used to put my soccer trophies on it. She said we could use the shelf at our house," Dad said.

"What about your trophies?" asked Astrid.

Dad shrugged. "When we moved, I lost them all."

"What?" Astrid covered her mouth in alarm. "All of them? I'm sorry, Dad."

"Me too," Apollo said quietly.

Dad tried to smile, but he looked sad. "Thanks. I wish I still had them. But now at least I'll have the shelf."

"Where will we put it?" asked Astrid.

"It should fit on the wall upstairs. But I'm not sure what to put *on* it yet," Dad said.

"We can help you think of something," Apollo said.

"Thanks!" said Dad. "There's Auntie Xai now."

Auntie Xai was walking toward them carrying the parts of the shelf. She had the boards and brackets to hang them on the wall.

Dad got out of the car to help. He took the parts and opened the trunk.

Auntie Xai waved to Astrid and Apollo through the car window. They waved back. Dad and Auntie Xai chatted outside.

All of a sudden, Astrid said, "Apollo, I know what we can put on the shelf!"

"What?" Apollo asked. He was curious to hear her idea.

"If we practice really hard, we can win trophies at the tournament. We can put *our* trophies on the shelf!" said Astrid.

"And since Dad lost all his trophies, ours will make him feel better," said Apollo. "Great idea, Astrid. Let's surprise Dad!"

CHAPTER 2

Practice Makes Perfect

Dad was ready to hang the shelf on the wall. Apollo stood next to him. His job was to help Dad.

Astrid and Mom stood in the hallway. Their job was to make sure the shelf was put up straight.

Eliana and their dog, Luna, stood next to them. Their job was to watch.

"How does it look?" Dad asked. He held one side of the shelf. Apollo held the other.

Astrid and Mom moved back.
Now they could see the whole wall.
They tilted their heads to the right.

"Go up on the right," said Astrid.

Eliana patted Luna and said,
"Right!"

Apollo moved the right side up.

Astrid and Mom tilted their heads
to the left.

"Now go up on the left," said
Mom.

"Left!" Eliana said as she scratched
behind Luna's ears.

Dad moved the left side up.

"Looks good," said Mom.

"It's great," said Astrid.

"Good! Great!" said Eliana.

Luna's ears perked up.

"Teamwork!" said Dad.

Dad used the drill to secure the
shelf to the wall. When he was
done, he said, "Now we just need
something to put on it."

Astrid and Apollo looked at each
other and smiled.

* * * * *

Later that evening, Apollo asked, "Can we practice in the living room?"

"Tae kwon do?" Mom said.

"Yes. Practice makes perfect," said Astrid.

Dad looked around the room and said, "Sure, but try not to break anything."

"Yes, be careful," Mom agreed.

Eliana pointed a finger at them. "Careful!" she repeated.

"Let's move this out of the way," said Dad.

He and Mom carried the coffee table away from the couch. The twins helped them push the couch against the wall.

Now there was a big, open space in the middle of the room.

"Yay!" said Eliana. She ran across the floor. Luna chased her. Mom picked up Eliana. Dad picked up Luna.

"Okay, tae kwon do champions," Mom said.

"The room is all yours," said Dad.

He and Mom walked to the kitchen with Eliana as she screamed, "Cham-pee-ons!"

* * * * *

"Let's do forms first," said Astrid. After kicks, forms were her favorite. She was good at remembering all the steps in the right order.

"You go first," Apollo said.

Astrid stood straight and bowed. She put her feet together and made fists. She took a step forward and pushed one arm out. Then she turned and punched with her fist. She yelled, "Heeyah!"

"Great job, Astrid!" said Apollo.

"Thanks!" Astrid said. "Your turn."

Apollo practiced the forms too. Then they both practiced them together.

When they were done, Astrid said, "Now let's do kicks! Do you want to go first?"

"Sure," said Apollo. He put up his fists. He bent his knee and kicked forward.

He yelled, "Heeyah!" He kicked again, turning his foot sideways. Then he leaned to the side and kicked straight out. "Heeyah!"

"That's so good, Apollo!" said Astrid.

"Thanks! You go now," he said.

Astrid did the same kicks. Apollo watched.

"Nice!" he said.

When Astrid was done, Apollo asked, "Should we break boards?"

"But we don't have boards," said Astrid.

Apollo picked up a throw pillow from the couch. "We need to win trophies for Dad. Practice makes perfect," he said.

"You're right," said Astrid. She took the pillow from Apollo and held it out to him.

Apollo bent his elbows and hit the pillow hard with his fist. "Heeyah!"

The pillow dropped to the floor, and they both fell over laughing.

CHAPTER 3

Tournament Day

It was the day of the tournament. Astrid and Apollo were so excited they could barely eat breakfast.

"Eat more kao pia," Mom said.

Astrid swallowed the soft rice noodles. But her stomach felt funny. She could only eat a little.

Apollo tapped his fingers on the table.

Eliana shoved kao pia into her mouth. Then she tried to tap the table like Apollo. Mom stopped her.

"Is something wrong?" Dad asked them.

"I just don't feel hungry," said Astrid.

"Me neither," said Apollo.

"Try to eat a little," said Mom. "You have a big day. Breakfast is important."

"Okay," they both said.

Astrid couldn't finish her bowl, but Apollo finished his. Then he got another bowl. He gulped down the noodles and asked, "Can I have one more bowl?"

Then Mom said, "Don't eat *too much* or you'll be too full!"

Astrid and Apollo laughed.

* * * * *

It was time to change into their tae kwon do uniforms. Astrid and Apollo went upstairs. They saw Dad's shelf in the hall. It was still empty.

"It will look better with our trophies on it," Apollo whispered.

Astrid nodded. "Yes, I hope I win a trophy!"

"You will! You're the best at forms in our class," said Apollo.

Astrid smiled. "Thanks, and you're the best at board breaking! So we'll both win trophies today. For Dad."

* * * * *

Dad drove the family to the high school. The tae kwon do tournament was being held in the school gym.

In the parking lot, they saw kids going into the building with their parents. They were all wearing white tae kwon do uniforms, just like Astrid and Apollo.

"Let me take a picture," Dad said when Astrid and Apollo got out of the car. "Are you feeling good?" he asked as they posed for the picture.

"I'm fine!" said Apollo.

Astrid nodded, but she was getting nervous.

Astrid and Apollo walked into the school with their family. They saw a line of kids waiting to check in. A big chart with the schedule hung on the wall.

Astrid saw FORMS listed first on the schedule. She was competing in that event, so she would go first. She sighed.

Apollo saw BOARD BREAKING on the chart. "I go after you," he said to Astrid. Then he turned and said, "There's Master Leon!"

Astrid looked in the gym. Master Leon was by the gym doors talking to some students.

"Are you okay?" asked Apollo. "You look worried."

Astrid shook her head. "I don't know."

"But you're the best at forms, remember?" said Apollo.

"Thanks," said Astrid, shrugging.

Dad and Apollo went to the table to check in.

Mom leaned down to Astrid and said, "You are excellent at forms. I don't want you to worry, Gao Nou. Try to have fun today."

"I want to win a trophy," said Astrid.

Mom nodded. "Winning is nice. But try to focus on tae kwon do. Think about how much you enjoy it—not just about winning."

"Okay," said Astrid.

But still, she wanted a trophy. She remembered when Dad said he lost his trophies. He was so sad. She wanted to put her trophy on the shelf so he could be happy.

Dad and Apollo came back, and they all walked into the gym together.

It was noisy and crowded. Families sat in rows of chairs. In the middle of the gym were big colored mats. Judges waited at long tables by the wall.

"We need to find the forms section," said Mom.

"Right there. That word means forms." Astrid pointed to a sign that read POOMSE.

Kids were practicing punches and kicks on the mats. Astrid started shaking. She didn't want to be there anymore. Tae kwon do class was fun, but this wasn't class.

This was making her nervous!

She was about to say she wanted to go home when Master Leon saw them.

"Astrid and Apollo Lee! My favorite tae kwon do twins!" he said.

He walked up to them. He said hello to Mom and Dad, and he smiled at Eliana.

Master Leon looked at Astrid. "Are you ready, Astrid?"

She didn't feel ready, but she nodded.

"Don't be nervous. Remember what we learned in class. You can do it!" Master Leon punched the air.

Astrid and Apollo laughed.

Master Leon smiled and walked away.

Mom and Eliana found chairs near the poomse mats. They sat down, and Mom said, "Good luck!"

"Thanks, Mom," said Astrid.

Then Dad said, "Wait, I want a family picture!"

Astrid and Apollo stood next to Mom, Dad, and Eliana. Dad held out his arm and took a picture of all of them together. Then he and Apollo walked with Astrid to the judges' table.

Astrid took a deep breath.

"You'll be great, Astrid," Apollo said.

Astrid nodded and looked at the table. She saw a big, shiny trophy. Next to the trophy was a plaque. Next to the plaque was a medal.

What if I don't get the trophy? she wondered.

Dad put his arm around her shoulder. "We're proud of you!" he whispered.

Astrid smiled. Then Apollo and Dad went to sit down.

CHAPTER 4

For Dad

A judge looked for Astrid's name on his list. He told her she would go last.

Astrid saw chairs next to the mats. The kids practicing before were now sitting in the seats, waiting for their turn. She went to sit with them.

Then the forms competition began. The first kid to go was a small boy. His name was Owen.

Owen's punches were fast. His yells were loud. When Owen was done, everyone clapped.

After that, a tall girl with long hair walked onto the mat. Astrid didn't know her name, but she looked strong. She moved quickly. Her kicks were the highest Astrid had ever seen.

When the tall girl was done, she returned to her seat. Now there were only five kids left.

Astrid tried to think about how much she liked tae kwon do. She tried not to think about winning. But she couldn't help it. The trophy was shining at her from the table.

Suddenly, the judges called her name.

Astrid stepped onto the mat. She stood straight and looked over at her family. Mom smiled, Dad gave her a thumbs-up, and Eliana waved.

Apollo nodded. Astrid knew that meant, *You can do it!*

Astrid bowed. Then she began.

She made fists. She moved one leg out. She punched. She yelled, "Heeyah!" But her yell was so soft, she couldn't even hear it! She would yell louder the next time.

Astrid turned and stepped forward with one foot. That's when she forgot what came next. Was it put your fist to your shoulder? Put your hand by your waist? Punch down, or punch straight?

Astrid froze. She looked at the judges. They were watching her.

Her heart was beating fast. She didn't know what to do. Finally, she remembered the next step. She kicked and did another punch, yelling, "Heeyah!" again, louder this time. She put her feet together and bowed. Everyone clapped.

Astrid went back to her chair. The judges thanked everyone. They compared notes for several minutes. Then they picked up the awards and began to name the winners.

The boy named Owen won the medal. The next award was for the plaque. Astrid closed her eyes tight and wished for the trophy.

"Astrid Lee!" the judge called out.

Astrid's eyes popped open. She tried not to look disappointed. But she had really wanted the trophy, not the plaque. She put on a small smile and went to accept her award.

Astrid saw Master Leon looking at her from across the gym. She quickly looked away and hurried over to Mom.

Mom hugged her. Astrid looked down at the floor. She had won the plaque, but she didn't feel like a winner.

"Astrid, you were amazing!" Apollo said.

Mom rubbed Astrid's back. "You were wonderful, honey."

Eliana hugged her too. "Good Astrid!" she said.

Astrid tried to catch her breath. "I forgot what to do."

"It's okay, Gao Nou," Dad said. "I'll go get you a coconut juice."

He headed off into the crowd, then Eliana began to run after him.

"Be right back," said Mom as she chased after Eliana.

"I didn't win the trophy!" Astrid said to Apollo. "Now I don't have a trophy for Dad."

"You got the plaque. And you tried your best. That counts!" said Apollo.

But Astrid shook her head. "I lost."

"I didn't see anyone lose up there," someone said.

They turned around. Master Leon was standing by their chairs.

Astrid stood up and said, "Master Leon, I'm sorry about the poomse. I practiced hard. I didn't mean to forget. And my first yell wasn't loud."

Master Leon smiled. "It was an incredible yell. What's important is you kept trying. That makes you brave."

"See! You *were* brave," said Apollo.

Master Leon patted Astrid's arm. "You *are* a winner! Awesome job!"

He looked at Apollo. "You're up next for breaking boards."

He gave Apollo a pat on the back and walked away.

"Can you win the trophy?" Astrid asked her brother.

"For Dad," said Apollo.

* * * * *

It was time to break boards. Apollo walked up to the mat. His stomach felt tight. His throat was dry.

He looked at the other kids in the competition. They looked so big. Were they fifth graders?

The judge found Apollo's name on the list, but he wouldn't go last like Astrid had. The judge told Apollo he was going first!

Apollo saw a man walk onto the mat. He was carrying a pile of small wooden boards. Apollo's eyes grew wide. *Wooden boards?* He swallowed. He tried not to get nervous.

Then it was time to start. Apollo took off his shoes and stepped onto the mat.

The man held up a board and nodded at Apollo.

Apollo ran to the board.

"Heeyah!" he yelled as he banged his hand against the wood.

He thought the board would crack. Every time he hit the foam boards in class, they broke right away.

But the wooden board dropped from the man's hand. It fell onto the mat, still in one piece.

The man picked it up. "Go again."

Apollo stepped back. He looked over at Astrid. She nodded.

Apollo ran to the board again and yelled, "Heeyah!" He slammed his hand into it. But the board still didn't break.

"One more time," said the man.

Apollo stepped back again. He stared at the board. What if he didn't win the trophy either? Then they wouldn't have any trophies for Dad's shelf.

Apollo kept his eyes on the board. He had to break it. This was his last chance! He bent his elbow and made a fist. He punched at the board as hard as he could! He heard a cracking sound—but the wood didn't break.

The man held up the board. Apollo had only split it halfway. He tried not to let his feelings show on his face. He bowed to the man and left the mat.

When the judges gave out the awards, Apollo won the medal. He didn't win the trophy.

He walked back to his family. He sat on the chair and put his head in his hands.

Eliana hugged him.

"You did super, Apollo!" said Astrid.

"You were outstanding," said Dad.

Mom touched Apollo's hand. It was red. "Does it hurt?" she asked.

It did, but Apollo didn't want to say so. He shook his head.

Then he saw Master Leon coming over. Mom and Dad stood up to talk to him. Astrid and Apollo looked at each other.

"Maybe he's saying I did a bad job," Apollo whispered.

"But you didn't!" Astrid said.

Mom and Dad were nodding. Master Leon was pointing at the boards. He kept talking.

"I didn't break the board in half," Apollo sighed. "Astrid, what are we going to do? We don't have a trophy for Dad."

"But we have a medal and a plaque!" said Astrid. "Anyway, you're the best at breaking boards. Everyone in class knows it. Master Leon knows it. Who cares about trophies?"

"I can only break foam boards, not wooden boards," Apollo said.

"We've never used wooden boards before. Bet if we did, you would have won the trophy! I still think you're the board-breaking champ," said Astrid.

"I don't feel like I am," said Apollo.

"You are!" Master Leon said.

Astrid and Apollo looked up.

Master Leon sat down in the chair next to Apollo.

"I was telling your parents this is your first time with wooden boards. And you still split the board!" he said.

"You were fantastic!" Mom said.

"You did a terrific job, Nou Kou," said Dad.

Master Leon nodded. "In tae kwon do, I teach you to work hard, try your best, and never give up."

He looked at Astrid. "You are both good students. You showed me today that you don't give up, even when things are tough. That makes you strong and brave."

Master Leon stood up. "To me, you are true tae kwon do champions."

CHAPTER 5

Family Award

When they got home, Astrid and Apollo were so tired. They went straight to the couch and sat down. They knew it was time to talk to Dad.

Luna was barking, so Dad opened her kennel. She jumped out and hopped onto the couch next to Astrid. Mom and Eliana followed her.

Astrid held Luna in her lap and said, "Dad, we're sorry."

"What?" Dad asked in surprise. He walked over. "Why?"

"We wanted to make you happy," said Astrid.

Dad smiled. "You *do* make me happy."

Astrid gave her plaque to Dad. Then Apollo handed him his medal. He said, "We really wanted to get trophies for your shelf. But we didn't win any."

"Is that why you wanted to win?" Mom asked.

"For the shelf?" Dad asked.

Astrid and Apollo nodded.

Dad looked at Mom, then turned back to Astrid and Apollo. "Wait here," he said.

Then he and Mom went upstairs.

Eliana sat between Astrid and Apollo. Luna crawled from Astrid's lap, over Eliana, and then onto Apollo's lap. They all laughed.

"You still sad?" Eliana asked them.

"I'm better now, thanks," said Astrid.

"Me too," said Apollo.

Eliana hugged them and sang a happy song.

After a few minutes, Mom came down the stairs and said, "Dad wants everyone to come upstairs, please!"

Astrid and Apollo looked at each other and shrugged. They followed Eliana and Luna up the stairs.

At the end of the hallway, Dad was standing in front of the shelf. "I want to show you something," he said.

When they got closer, Dad said, "Thank you for wanting to give me trophies, since I lost mine. But I have something better than any trophy now."

He moved to the side. Three framed pictures sat on the self.

There was a picture of Astrid and Apollo standing by the car in their white uniforms.

Next to that was a picture of the family together in the gym at the tournament.

Last of all, there was a picture of Eliana and Luna, snuggling together.

"My family is the best award ever," Dad said.

Astrid and Apollo smiled at each other. Dad didn't need trophies to be happy. He had *them*.

They went up to Dad.

Mom, Eliana, and Luna joined them. Then they shared the biggest family hug of all.

FACTS ABOUT THE HMONG

LAOS

- Hmong people first lived in southern China. Many of them moved to Southeast Asia in the 1800s. Some Hmong decided to stay in the country of Laos (pronounced *LAH-ohs*).

- In the 1950s, a war called the Vietnam War started in Southeast Asia. The United States joined this war. They asked the Hmong in Laos to help them. When the U.S. lost the war, Hmong people had to leave Laos.

- After 1975, many Hmong came to the U.S. as refugees. Refugees are people who escape from their country to find a new, safe place to live. Today, Minnesota is home to around 85,000 Hmong.

- Many Hmong American families enjoy outdoor activities like camping, boating, and fishing.

bitter melon—a vegetable that looks like a bumpy cucumber and tastes very bitter. It is often cooked in Hmong soups and other dishes.

coconut juice—a drink made from the juice of young coconuts. Coconut juice comes in a can or a small box with a straw. This drink is enjoyed by many Hmong children.

fish sauce—a strong, salty sauce that is used as a seasoning for Hmong and other Southeast Asian dishes

kao pia—a noodle dish from Laos that many Hmong people enjoy. It is made of soft rice noodles in chicken broth. Sometimes the noodles can be short and round instead of long and thin.

pandan—a tropical plant used as a sweet flavoring in Southeast Asian cakes and desserts

pork and green vegetable soup—pork and leafy green vegetables boiled in a broth. This is a typical dish that Hmong families eat at mealtime.

rice in water—a bowl or plate of rice with water added to it. Many Hmong children and elderly Hmong people like to eat rice this way.

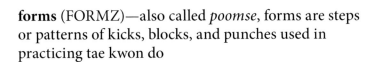

GLOSSARY

forms (FORMZ)—also called *poomse*, forms are steps or patterns of kicks, blocks, and punches used in practicing tae kwon do

judge (JUDJ)—a person who makes decisions in a contest or competition

nervous (NER-vuss)—feeling worried, scared, or anxious

plaque (PLACK)—a flat piece of board or metal with engraving that says what a person has won or achieved

poomse (POOM-say)—the Korean word for tae kwon do forms

schedule (SKEDJ-yuhl)—a listing of the order in which things happen

sparring (SPARR-ing)—a way for tae kwon do students to practice kicks, blocks, and punches with each other; students wear protective gear when sparring

tae kwon do (TIE KWAHN DOH)—a form of martial arts from Korea that uses different movements like kicks, jump kicks, blocks, and punches

tournament (TOUR-nuh-ment)—an important contest or competition

trophy (TROH-fee)—a small statue made of plastic or metal given as an award

V.T. Bidania has been writing stories ever since she was five years old. She was born in Laos and grew up in St. Paul, Minnesota, right where Astrid and Apollo live! She has an MFA in creative writing from The New School and is a McKnight Writing Fellow. She lives outside of the Twin Cities and spends her free time reading all the books she can find, writing more stories, and playing with her family's sweet Morkie.

ABOUT THE ILLUSTRATOR

Evelt Yanait is a freelance children's digital artist from Barcelona, Spain, where she grew up drawing and reading wonderful illustrated books. After working as a journalist for an NGO for many years, she decided to focus on illustration, her true passion. She loves to learn, write, travel, and watch documentaries, discovering and capturing new lifestyles and stories whenever she can. She also does social work with children and youth, and she's currently earning a Social Education degree.

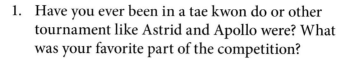

TALK ABOUT IT

1. Have you ever been in a tae kwon do or other tournament like Astrid and Apollo were? What was your favorite part of the competition?

2. Astrid and Apollo wanted to surprise Dad and give him their trophies. Explain why they wanted to do this.

3. What does "practice makes perfect" mean to you? What is something you practice really hard so you can do it well? Share how you practice it.

WRITE IT DOWN

1. Astrid was so nervous when she arrived at the tournament. Can you think of what she could have done to feel better? Write a list of things that might help a person feel calmer before competing.

2. What if Astrid and Apollo never told their dad the reason they wanted trophies? Pretend you are Astrid or Apollo and write a letter to Dad explaining why you were trying so hard to win.

3. Imagine you have a trophy shelf like Mr. Lee's. Write a paragraph or draw a picture of all the awards you would put on it. They can be real or imaginary!